STOP!

There's a snake in your suitcase!

Also by Adam Frost

Run! The Elephant Weighs a Ton!

*More animal adventures with the
Nightingale family coming soon!*

STOP!
There's a snake in your suitcase!

Adam Frost

Illustrated by
Mark Chambers

LONDON NEW DELHI NEW YORK SYDNEY

All of the animal facts in this story are true. Everything else is fiction. Any connection to any events that have taken place in London Zoo is purely coincidental.

Bloomsbury Publishing, London, New Delhi, New York and Sydney

First published in Great Britain in June 2012 by Bloomsbury Publishing Plc
50 Bedford Square, London, WC1B 3DP

Manufactured and supplied under licence from the Zoological Society of London

A CIP catalogue record for this book is available from the British Library

ISBN 978 1 4088 2706 2

MIX
Paper from
responsible sources
FSC® C018072

Typeset by Hewer Text UK Ltd, Edinburgh
Printed in Great Britain by Clays Ltd, St Ives Plc, Bungay, Suffolk

1 3 5 7 9 10 8 6 4 2

www.storiesfromthezoo.com
www.bloomsbury.com
www.adam-frost.com

To Leon

Chapter 1

'Keep up, slowcoach!' Tom Nightingale called over his shoulder to his best friend, Freddy Finch, as they skateboarded home from school on Thursday evening. 'Hey, shall we go through Regent's Park or along the canal?'

'Through the park,' Freddy shouted back. 'It's easier to do tricks in there.'

Thirty seconds later, and they were whizzing past the boating lake, stopping every few minutes to try kick-flips and ollies and a special trick that Tom had invented called a 'tiger's leap', which involved skateboarding towards a bench, leaping up on to the seat and running along it while your skateboard was rolling under the bench, and then jumping back on your board at the other end.

Tom had got the skateboard for his ninth birthday and had been practising every day since.

'Race you to the bandstand,' Freddy cried

'Hang on, it gets crowded over there . . .' Tom said.

But he might as well not have bothered as Freddy was already speeding off. 'You're just saying that cos you know you'll lose!' he shouted back over his shoulder.

Tom frowned. They'd see about that. He pushed off and gave chase. The two boys whizzed past the swings and weaved through Avenue Gardens. Freddy swerved right and raced past the open-air theatre and the outdoor cafe. As they rounded the corner by Clarence Bridge, Freddy swerved to avoid a pigeon and crashed into Tom's skateboard. Both boys flew through the air and landed on a patch of grass. Tom was

about to scramble to his feet, but Freddy was pointing at something under a nearby bush.

'Hey, Tom,' he called out, 'look at this.'

Tom stopped and turned round to see where Freddy was pointing.

'It's not a trick,' said his friend. 'Look, you've won, OK? Just come and see what I've found.'

Tom picked up his skateboard and walked over to where Freddy was sitting.

'Look – there . . .' Freddy pointed at a green shape under the bush. Tom squinted and made out a long green snake. A grass snake. It had wriggled around on to its back. It kept squirming for a few seconds and then it stopped moving and lay there completely still with its mouth open and its tongue hanging out. A drop of blood trickled from its mouth.

'I didn't touch it, honest!' said Freddy.

'What do you think is wrong with it?' Tom said, putting his hand into the bush.

'Don't touch it, you idiot. It might bite,' said Freddy.

'Grass snakes don't bite,' said Tom, gently stroking its stomach. 'It probably thinks you're going to bite him. I thought it would be cold and slimy, but it's sort of dry and warm.'

Freddy was raising one eyebrow. 'You and your family have way too much time for animals.' Then he raised both eyebrows. 'Hey, talking of your family, your sister will know what's wrong with it. She wants to be a vet like your mum, right?'

'Suppose I could ring her,' said Tom. He got a mobile phone out of his back pocket. 'I'm only meant to use it in emergencies.'

'This is an emergency,' Freddy said. 'He's on his last legs. Not that he's got any legs.'

Tom called his big sister, Sophie. The phone rang five times before she picked it up.

'OK, what have you done now?' she asked.

'Nothing,' Tom protested. 'Listen – me and Freddy found this snake.' He explained what he could see and then put his sister on speakerphone.

'Hmm,' Sophie said. There were a few seconds of silence and then she started speaking again. 'I suspect it's just playing dead. It's one of the ways that grass snakes react to predators. He'll emit a nasty-smelling liquid from his bottom in a minute.'

'Blimey!' Freddy said, holding his nose. 'He has as well.'

'It's to make you think he's rotting,' Sophie said. 'To put you off eating him.'

'Like I was about to tuck in,' Freddy muttered.

'Anyway, whatever you do, DON'T move him anywhere,' Sophie said. 'He'll be there for a reason. He's either warming up or cooling down. If you move him, he really could be in trouble.'

As soon as she said the word 'trouble', the snake flipped over on to its belly and slithered into the bush at lightning speed.

'Could you – I mean – did you – see that?' Freddy spluttered.

'All right, thanks, Soph,' Tom said. 'See you back on the barge.'

The boys got back on their skateboards and trundled along side by side.

'Here's what gets me,' said Freddy.

'What?' Tom asked.

'He's got no legs, no arms and yet he's as fast as a ferret running up someone's trouser leg.'

'Yeah.' Tom nodded.

'He's got no ears and no nose,' Freddy went on. 'And yet he had ninja reflexes.'

'I remember Dad saying that snakes sense things with their tongue,' Tom said. 'You know, how they flicker it in and out all the time. They pick up smells and movement and pass it back to their brains.'

'Blimey,' said Freddy. 'You mean like this?' He stuck his tongue out and started moving his skateboard in a snake-like fashion, weaving left and right.

Tom grinned and copied him and soon they were skating forward like a pair of snakes. They passed a mother wheeling her baby along in a pushchair.

She frowned at them. 'Rude boys,' she muttered. 'Don't pay any attention to them, Popsy.'

Tom and Freddy laughed out loud and then stuck their tongues back in again.

Chapter 2

Sophie had been on her way back from school with her best friend, Jemima, when Tom had called.

'So what was that all about?' Jemima asked as Sophie hung up. 'Has Simon just dumped you?'

Sophie groaned. 'How many times do I have to tell you, I'm not going out with Simon!'

'Try telling Simon that,' Jemima said. 'So what was it then?'

'It was Tom,' Sophie replied. 'He needed my help with a grass snake.'

'A grass snake?' said Jemima. 'Hang on a minute. I know that look!'

'What look?' said Sophie.

'The look you get when you hear about a lost or injured animal – sort of mushy,' said Jemima.

'What do you mean?' Sophie said.

'Just what I said.' Jemima laughed. 'You're thinking about snakes, aren't you?' Don't tell me you're thinking about getting one!'

'Well, no,' Sophie replied. 'Not exactly.'

'Sophie!'

'They're just interesting, that's all.'

The two girls turned along the road that led to Regent's Park. Sophie was twelve years old, but because she was tall and clever and confident she could easily pass for fourteen. Jemima was the same age, and also got mistaken for older, but this was mainly because of the dyed red hair and the mascara.

'My cousin has a snake

called Albert; they are the grossest pets ever,' said Jemima.

'Come on, there are grosser pets,' said Sophie. 'What about spiders? Or slugs?'

'It's got to be snakes,' said Jemima. 'Every time I go to my cousin's house, you open the fridge and there's a mouse defrosting in there. Albert's dinner!'

Sophie laughed.

'And he's always escaping,' said Jemima. 'One time, I was over there watching telly when I felt this arm creeping round my shoulder. You know, like I'm in the back row at the cinema. Only it wasn't an arm, it was Albert! I turn round and there I am – eyeball to eyeball with him.'

'What kind of snake is he?' asked Sophie.

'I don't know, do I?' said Jemima. 'A flippin' big one! With fangs! So look, if you get one, there's no way I'm coming over to your house again. Not that you've got a house, but you know what I mean.'

They stopped at a gate that led down to the Regent's Canal towpath. The houseboat that Sophie lived on with her family was moored on the canal below, whereas Jemima's house was a little further on up the hill.

'Don't worry,' said Sophie. 'I won't get a snake any time soon. For a start, I don't think Clarence and Win would like it very much.'

'Who are they? Your mice?'

'My rats,' said Sophie.

'Don't tell me,' said Jemima, scrunching up her eyes, 'rats are misunderstood as well. Talking of rats, look – it's Christian Hemmings. Stay with me.'

'But you used to like him.'

'That was when he was still washing his freaking hair.'

'Sorry, Jem, got dogs to walk, fish to feed.' Sophie smiled over her shoulder as she walked down the track that led to her boat. Jemima pulled a mock-angry face and then turned to face a sullen-looking teenage boy wearing eyeliner.

As Sophie got closer to the canal, she felt London fading away behind her. Within a few seconds there were no more car horns or police sirens; there was no music blaring from shops. She was surrounded by trees and water and wildlife.

She pulled out a crust of bread that she'd saved from her packed lunch and threw it towards a patch of reeds. A group of ducklings emerged, quacking happily and jabbing at the bread.

'All right, try not to fight over it,' she said. Sophie watched for a moment before walking on towards the marina, where the houseboats were moored.

As she passed the first boat she heard a voice coming out of an open porthole.

'Hello, Sophie. How's your mum?'

'Better now, thanks, Mrs Macready,' Sophie said, bending down to look in. 'It was just a bad cold.'

'Good, good,' said the voice. 'Send her my love.'

On the second boat there was a man on the bow, cooking sausages on a barbecue. He looked up and waved.

'Hi, Jim,' Sophie said.

'Can you give this screwdriver back to your dad?' he said, picking it up from the roof of the boat and handing it to her.

'Sure thing,' Sophie said.

She passed the third barge and waved at a middle-aged woman who was repainting the name of her boat on its prow: *LILY THE PINK*.

The woman turned round and said, 'Hello, Sophie. If you and Tom want to earn a tenner at the weekend, I could use a hand re-sanding the deck.'

'Call it twenty and you've got a deal,' Sophie said.

'Fifteen and as many muffins as you can eat!' said the woman with a smile.

'Done,' said Sophie.

After walking past another three barges, Sophie finally reached the family boat.

All of the boats on the canal were completely different to each other – some were black and long, while others were short and blue. There were red ones and green ones – some brand new, others old-fashioned. Some of them were built for one person, others could hold ten. But even in the midst of all this variety, the Nightingale boat really stood out.

For a start, half the roof had been turned into a vegetable garden, while the other half was covered with solar panels. Then there was the boat itself, which was decorated all over with animals. Tom and Sophie's dad had painted rhinos, bears, tigers, zebras and lots of other creatures on the sides. The portholes had been worked into the design as well, so that if you were inside, looking out, you could be poking out of a kangaroo's pouch, stuck inside a lion's mouth or peering out of a tortoise's shell.

Inside there were animals everywhere too. The family had a terrier called Rex and two cats called Mindy and Max, while Tom had five stick insects and Sophie had her two rats, a ferret, a budgie and eleven goldfish.

The boat's name was the *Jessica Rose*. But everyone in the marina just called it *The Ark*.

Sophie opened the front door and ducked inside. Rex had come running out of his basket as soon as he heard the key turn in the lock. Sophie swept him up and screwed up her face as he licked her chin.

'Ready for walkies, Rexie?' she asked. Rex leapt out of her arms and stood in front of the hook where his lead was hanging.

'OK, let's take Felicity as well,' she said.

She picked up a small collar from the window-sill and walked over to her ferret's cage.

Within a couple of minutes, Rex the terrier and Felicity the ferret were on their way to Regent's Park, pulling Sophie along behind them.

Chapter 3

While Sophie was taking the animals for a walk, Tom was on his way down to the canal. He was still thinking about the grass snake that he and Freddy had seen. He wondered if there were any other snakes in this part of London and how easy it would be to spot them. He decided to ask Grandad about it.

Grandad lived in a houseboat at the other end of the marina – which was very handy for everyone. Before he'd retired, he had been Chief Vet at London Zoo, just as his daughter, Tom's mum, was now also Chief Vet there. In fact, the whole family worked at the zoo – Tom's dad was a keeper there too.

As Tom put his skateboard down on the towpath he saw his sister coming towards him, pulled by Rex and Felicity.

'So, did the snake survive?' she asked.

Rex was jumping up on Tom's trousers.

'Yeah, I think he was fine,' said Tom, stroking Rex. 'In fact, I was on my way to ask Grandad about it now. And about snakes in general.'

'Well, ask him about keeping one as a pet too, will you?' Sophie said, 'I'm thinking about getting one.'

'A big scary one?' Tom asked. 'A huge long venomous one? I saw one on TV that dislocated its jaw and swallowed a whole crocodile.'

'That would be a boa constrictor,' said Sophie. 'Probably *not* one like that.'

'Oh,' said Tom, disappointed.

A moment later, a houseboat glided past them, steering towards the bank.

'Did I hear someone mention snakes?' a voice called out.

Tom and Sophie turned round. The voice was coming from the houseboat. A tall thin man stood on the deck with a grin on his face and a thick snake around his neck. The snake twisted its head round and fixed Tom and Sophie with its black beady eyes, flicking its tongue in and out.

Rex growled and stood behind Sophie.

'Whoa, is that a boa constrictor?' Tom called out.

'A Burmese python actually,' the man said, grinning. 'Fancy a stroke?'

Sophie stared at the snake. Something about it puzzled her. She couldn't help noticing a couple of sores on its skin and a swelling on the side of its head. Why was it in such a bad condition?

She turned to look at the man. He had a scar on his cheek and about six teeth in his mouth. His arms and neck were covered in tattoos. They were smudged and wobbly and Sophie remembered Jemima telling her about tattoos that people got in prison.

'Look who's down here having a swim,' the man said.

He pulled another snake out of a cage that was trailing in the canal. This one was green with black spots and extremely long.

'Blimey, what's that?' Tom asked.

'It looks like an anaconda,' said Sophie.

The man dropped the snake back in the cage with a splash.

'Clever girl,' said the man. 'Got all sorts in here. Cobras, rattlesnakes . . . you name it. Plus some other reptiles: iguanas, chameleons, turtles.'

'But there can't be enough room,' said Sophie.

'There ain't,' the man said. 'That's why I'm selling 'em. Now this boa would cost you around two thousand pounds on the open market, but you can have it for a monkey.'

'But we don't own a monkey,' said Tom.

The man chuckled. 'A monkey means five hundred pounds, son. Go and get your mum or dad and we'll seal the deal right here, right now.'

'We're fine, thanks,' Sophie said decisively. 'We don't need any more animals.'

The man looked up and down the canal.

'You're breaking my heart here, sweetheart. All right, a rattlesnake for a pony. That's twenty-five nicker.'

His sales patter was interrupted when an old man holding a walking stick appeared next to Tom and Sophie.

'What's going on here?' he said, patting Rex on the head.

'Oh, hi, Grandad,' said Tom.

'Can I swap a pony for a snake?'

Tom and Sophie's grandad looked up at the man on the barge. 'Buying and selling, are you?' Then he let out a low whistle. 'My word!' he said, pointing with his cane. 'Look at the condition of that snake! And is that captive-bred? It looks like a wild snake to me!'

'Keep your voice down, old man,' the man snarled.

'I will not keep my voice down,' said Grandad. 'If I'm not mistaken, those are smuggled animals, aren't they? Sophie, do you have one of those modern portable telephones? I'm calling the police.'

'Don't you dare,' said the old man, 'unless you want a king cobra down your trousers!'

'Are you threatening me?' barked Grandad. 'What else do you have in that boat?'

'He said turtles, Grandad,' Sophie said, handing him her mobile. 'Iguanas, chameleons . . . all sorts of stuff.'

But the man had already turned his engine on and was steering the boat away from the bank.

'Oh no you don't,' Grandad called after him, waving a fist in the air. He stared at the phone. 'So how do you work it, Sophie? There aren't any buttons, just a screen. It doesn't make any sense.'

As the man and his houseboat moved off down the canal, Sophie took the phone back and dialled 999.

'He won't get far,' Grandad said. 'He's using the worst getaway vehicle in the world! His top speed in that houseboat will be five miles per hour!'

'I just hope the animals are OK,' said Sophie.

'A man like that belongs in a zoo!' growled Grandad, as the houseboat rounded a curve in the canal.

'I wouldn't let him anywhere near a zoo,' murmured Sophie.

A voice crackled on the other end of her mobile phone.

'Hello,' Sophie said, holding the phone up to her ear, 'can you put me through to the police, please? This is an emergency.'

Chapter 4

Tom, Sophie and their grandad stood side by side on the bank, staring at the houseboat as it made its way down the river.

Then Tom whispered to Sophie, 'I'm going to chase him.'

Sophie whispered back, 'What are you talking about? Don't be an idiot!'

'He'll get away if we don't do something!' Tom said. 'You should come too.' He turned to Grandad. 'I'll come and see you later, Grandad. Me and Sophie have urgent business to attend to.'

'Who's Sergeant Peters?' Grandad said, cupping his hand around his good ear.

'Not Sergeant Peters — URGENT BUSINESS,' Tom said. He put his skateboard down on the towpath and Rex hopped on the front.

As Tom pushed off, Sophie sighed and followed him, Felicity scampering along beside her.

As they turned the corner of the canal, they passed London Zoo, where their parents worked. The canal cut the zoo in two, with owls and toucans and a giant aviary on the north side of the canal and giraffes and zebras and all the other zoo animals on the south side. Two bridges linked the two sides of the zoo.

Tom and Sophie passed underneath the first bridge at exactly the same moment as their mother and father walked over it. Mr and Mrs Nightingale had just finished their shifts at the zoo — Mrs Nightingale worked in the zoo

26

hospital and Mr Nightingale worked in the large-mammals section.

Mr Nightingale spotted Tom and Sophie on the towpath below.

'Tom! Sophie!' he called out.

But they were too busy talking to each other to hear him.

'They're up to something,' Mr Nightingale said to his wife. 'Tom had that look in his eye.'

'You mean the don't-talk-to-me-I'm-on-a-mission look?' said Mrs Nightingale. 'Yes, I know the one. It always reminds me of you, for some reason.'

'Well, I'd better see what they're doing,' said Mr Nightingale, jogging away from his wife. 'Besides, it'd be a shame to miss out on the fun.'

Tom and Sophie passed the other zoo bridge. Usually they'd stop to peer up at the birds in the aviary, but not today.

'There he is,' said Tom. 'I can see the back of his boat.'

'We'd better keep our distance,' Sophie said, 'or he'll see us.'

Rex was still balancing on the front of Tom's skateboard. Now Tom had slowed down, the little terrier hopped off and started trotting along the towpath again.

'Your skateboard's pretty noisy, you know,' Sophie said. 'He'll hear it if you're not careful.'

'You're right.' Tom picked up his board and put it under his arm. 'What time did the police say they'd get here?'

'They didn't,' said Sophie as they walked briskly along the towpath, sticking close to the bushes.

'Quick! Hide! He's looking this way!' Tom exclaimed.

They both ducked down behind a bin.

'Someone's chucked away a whole packet of Cheestrings,' Tom said.

'Do NOT eat them!' hissed Sophie.

'They've not even been opened!' protested Tom.

'Shh, he's speeding up,' Sophie said.

The houseboat started to move more quickly. Tom and Sophie had to run to keep up with it.

'He's shouting at someone on the bank,' said Tom.

The houseboat was going at maximum speed now. Soon Tom had to stop to get his breath back.

'You . . . keep . . . going,' he gasped. 'Will catch . . . up . . . on . . . skay . . . board.'

'OK, keep Rex and Felicity with you,' said Sophie.

Tom bent over for a few moments to catch his breath, Rex on one side of him and Felicity on the other.

Sophie picked up the pace. She was one of the fastest runners in her school, particularly over short distances, so she had no problem keeping up with the houseboat.

She passed an old couple out for an early evening stroll.

'Hello, Mr Davies, Mrs Davies,' she panted as the houseboat on the canal slid in between two others that were heading in the opposite direction.

Sophie continued to run as quickly as she could.

Then she saw the man balancing on the roof of the houseboat. He was peering down at the bank. Then he threw three large objects into the bushes and jumped back down on to the deck.

Sophie reached the spot where he had thrown the objects. They looked like two pillowcases and a suitcase. The suitcase was tangled up in a hedge. One pillowcase was sitting in the middle of the towpath and the other was perched on the very edge of the towpath, about to drop into the canal.

Instinctively Sophie picked up the pillowcase that was at the edge of the path and threw it towards the hedge for safety. It made a loud hissing noise, just as Tom's skateboard appeared behind her.

'What happened? What's wrong?' he asked.

Rex barked at the pillowcases while Felicity sniffed at one of them and then backed away.

'He's dumped this stuff,' Sophie said, nodding at the pillowcases and the suitcase.

'What's in them?' Tom asked.

'Well, I heard hissing,' Sophie said, 'so I'm guessing snakes.'

Tom approached the pillowcase on the towpath and prodded it gingerly with his toe.

'Tom, what are you doing?' Sophie cried out.

A king cobra reared up out of the pillowcase. Its hood was open and it was leaning back, ready to strike.

'Get back! Get back!' Sophie screamed.

Tom fell over backwards and landed on the towpath with a *thump*.

The cobra darted its head forwards and then backwards, threatening to bite.

Sophie grabbed Tom by the armpits and dragged him backwards as quickly as she could. She picked up Rex and Felicity's leads and yanked them back too.

'A cobra bite can kill you in twenty minutes,' she whispered.

'I'm OK, I'm OK. He didn't bite me,' said Tom.

'You mean, he hasn't . . . *yet*,' said Sophie. 'We need to get further back – some cobras can spit venom into your eyes and blind you.'

The cobra was starting to emerge from the pillowcase. Its top half disappeared into the hedge; its bottom half was still sliding across the towpath. It was five metres long at least.

'It's escaping!' Tom cried. 'What do we do?'

'Don't move. I'm ringing Dad's mobile,' said Sophie, at the same time as a ringing tone came from behind them.

'Dad? Dad!' she cried as her father appeared by her side.

'Hello, kids,' he said. 'What's going on here?'

Then he saw the bottom half of the king cobra sticking out of the hedge.

'Have you been bitten?' he asked anxiously.

'No,' Tom and Sophie said.

'OK, get right back over there. Behind that tree,' he ordered them.

As they backed away, Mr Nightingale groaned quietly. 'Why can't you just find stray kittens – like *normal children*?'

Chapter 5

Within five minutes, the towpath was swarming with zookeepers, vets, police officers and fire-fighters.

Tom and Sophie were sitting on the branch of a tree about twenty metres away, watching it all. Rex and Felicity were tied to the bottom of the tree.

Tom and Sophie saw how the zookeepers had special equipment to handle the snakes.

One of the snakes was picked up with a pair of long-handled tongs and dropped carefully into a box.

Another longer snake was picked up with two

huge metal hooks that were tucked under his belly and then used to gently carry him into another box. His middle section hung down loosely between the two hooks.

Most of the keepers that were handling the snakes wore a large black glove on one of their hands.

'I've read about those gloves,' said Sophie. 'They're made of special material. Snakes can't smell your skin through them. If they bite you, their fangs can't get through either.'

The keepers were putting some of the snakes in boxes near the canal. Others were placed in boxes next to the trees.

'Why have they separated out the snakes like that?' Tom asked.

'Looks like they're keeping the two types in different places,' Sophie explained. 'I think those ones are venomous and these ones here are non-venomous.'

She pointed at the collection of boxes and bags nearest the tree they were sitting in.

'So these snakes can't kill us?' Tom asked.

'Oh yeah,' Sophie said, 'they can definitely do that. Only not with a bite – just by squeezing our guts out! It's called constriction.'

'Wow,' said Tom. He thought for a moment. 'I wonder what would be worse – being squeezed to death or getting bitten.'

'Hmm,' said Sophie. 'Getting bitten by, say, a cobra would mean that you may be paralysed in ten minutes. Then your lungs would pack up. Then you'd die.'

'And what about being constricted?' Tom asked.

'Well, the snake coils itself round you and slowly squeezes until you stop breathing. Then it stretches its jaw round your legs and starts swallowing you whole.'

'Cool!' exclaimed Tom. 'That sounds way better. I'm going to ask Dad to show me some of the constrictors.'

'I don't know if he will . . .' Sophie said.

'But we found them!' Tom protested. 'They're basically ours, aren't they?'

Sophie was looking at her mother and the group of vets that were peering at the snakes in their boxes.

'I just hope those snakes are OK,' said Sophie. 'Some of them looked really sick.'

At that moment, her phone rang. 'Mum' flashed up on the screen. Sophie could see Mrs Nightingale holding her phone about thirty metres away.

'Sophie, where are you? Is Tom with you?' she asked.

'Yeah, look up,' said Sophie. She waved. 'Wave at Mum, Tom.' Tom waved.

'Get down from there,' Mrs Nightingale said. 'You shouldn't be so close to all this.'

'OK, keep your hair on,' said Sophie.

'You'll have to have dinner at Grandad's tonight,' Mrs Nightingale said. 'The snakes are coming to the zoo, so your dad and I could be a while.'

Sophie hung up and said, 'Yesss – dinner at Grandad's!'

'Yesss,' said Tom.

Dinner at Grandad's meant takeaway pizza.

Tom and Sophie dropped Rex and Felicity back at *The Ark*. Then they made their way to Grandad's houseboat, the *Molly Magee*.

Tom grabbed the rope that hang down from the brass bell by the front door and rang it loudly.

Quickly they told Grandad everything that had happened.

'Lovely creatures, snakes,' Grandad said, as they waited for the pizzas to arrive. 'Never understood why people hate them so much.'

'I don't hate them,' said Sophie.

'Nor do I,' said Tom.

'That's because you've got brains in your heads,' said Grandad. 'If you believe what you read in books, it's very different. In the Bible, all the evil in the world is because of a snake. The devil turns into a snake and tempts Adam and Eve in the Garden of Eden. And look at all the old myths: the Hydra, whose top half was just dozens of snakes, Medusa with her snakes for hair . . .'

'Snakes for hair?' exclaimed Tom. 'Excellent. I'd like to see Mum try to brush that.'

'Thing is,' Grandad said, 'all of these stories are unfair to snakes. They're pretty shy and gentle really. They'll only bite you if you bother them. And if you bother snakes, then you deserve all you get!'

Tom's stomach started to rumble.

'Years ago, before I became a vet,' Grandad said, leaning back in his chair, 'I spent a year in Texas, researching rattlesnakes. They're fabulous creatures. Every time they shed their skin, they get another segment on their rattle. Did you know that? So the young ones are completely silent. And the old ones are very loud. Can you think of any other species like that?' He roared with laughter.

'Now, in Texas,' he continued, 'some of the locals did this thing called a rattlesnake round-up. It was totally barbaric! They hunted and killed hundreds of rattlesnakes every year, just for fun! Anyway, one time I was just watching one male rattler, when I saw a local spring out of the brush and chop its head clean off. And you know what happened? When he leant down to inspect it, the head twisted round and bit him. Ha ha! Bet he didn't see that coming! you see. Anyway, I couldn't save the snake, but I saved his mate. She gave birth to seven splendid little snakelets the following week.'

'What happened to the man?' Tom asked.

'Oh, I gave him some antivenin,' said Grandad, 'but only after he'd promised never to hurt a snake again.' He burst out laughing again.

'You didn't!' Sophie exclaimed with a grin.

'I certainly did,' said Grandad.

There was a knock on the door.

'Splendid,' said Grandad.

He went to answer it and came back with three cardboard boxes of pizza.

'Three ham and pineapples with extra olives, anchovies and spicy beef,' he said 'Dinner is served!'

Chapter 6

The following day was a Saturday. This meant one thing for Tom and Sophie – a day at the zoo.

Tom woke up first. He and Sophie had their own rooms on the boat, but they were quite small, and the walls between them were thin, so it was possible for Tom in his bed to talk to Sophie in her bed without raising his voice.

'Soph, are you awake?' Tom asked, staring up at the ceiling of his room.

'No,' groaned Sophie through the wall.

'How do snakes sleep?' Tom asked. 'Can they shut their eyes?'

'I'm not sure,' said Sophie. 'Hang on – they

can't, because they've got no eyelids. I suppose they just curl up and stop moving.'

'When a snake's asleep,' said a sleepy voice from their parents' room, 'they won't react to anything. You can move an object in front of their pupils and they won't look at it.'

It was Mrs Nightingale.

'Now go back to sleep, it's far too early,' she added.

Tom lasted another ten seconds, staring at the ceiling and trying not to talk.

Then he asked, 'You know all those snakes we found? Will they be there in the reptile house today?'

'Of course not, you dummy,' Sophie said.

'Sophie!' Mrs Nightingale exclaimed. 'Don't be mean to your brother.'

'They're in quarantine, mate,' said Mr Nightingale. 'They have to be checked for diseases and kept separate from the other snakes. For a good few months. Now go back to sleep, or we'll put you in quarantine too.'

'Really, Dad? Really?' Tom exclaimed. 'Can I go in quarantine with the snakes?'

'Flipping heck, Ed,' said Mrs Nightingale. 'That was hardly going to quieten him down.'

Everybody accepted that the day had begun.

After getting washed and dressed, the family assembled in the living room for breakfast.

Mrs Nightingale sliced some bread and put it under the grill. Mr Nightingale and the children turned the living room into a dining room. They slid the sofa into the wall and pushed the TV into its cabinet. They flipped out the dining table from under the window and unfolded four collapsible chairs. They slid a small shelf into a slot above the table and placed the jam and honey on it.

Mr Nightingale had built most of this furniture himself, because normal tables and cupboards were nearly always too big to fit neatly into a houseboat.

Sophie picked up the two bottles of milk that

had been left by the milkman on the towpath outside. She poured some into a saucer for the cats.

As the family munched toast and crunched cereal, Tom asked more questions.

'So how big is the biggest snake in the world? And how many ribs do they have? How can you tell if it's a girl or a boy?'

'Tom, it's a bit early for this,' Mr Nightingale said, scratching his head. 'Save up all your questions and we'll answer them later.'

'Or type them into Google,' said Sophie, yawning.

Tom tried a different approach. 'So how long is quarantine then? When can we see the snakes? Do they have names yet? Can one of them be called Tom, because I found them?'

Their mum smiled. 'You can't see the snakes just yet,' she said, 'but when the quarantine period is over, they'll probably join the zoo collection and you'll be able to meet them properly.'

'When will that be though?' asked Tom. 'Next week? The week after? I might be bored of snakes by then. I might be into pigs or chimps or something.'

'If only . . .' Mr Nightingale said, pouring himself more coffee.

Half an hour later, the Nightingales said good-bye to all the animals on *The Ark* and headed to the zoo. They walked along the towpath, over the bridge, along the edge of Regent's Park and through the staff turnstile.

Mr Nightingale went to the large-mammals section and Mrs Nightingale went to the zoo hospital. This left Tom and Sophie free to explore.

Tom was still slightly grumpy when they first arrived, but a morning at the zoo soon cheered him up.

First up was 'Into Africa'. Tom and Sophie looked at giraffes and zebras and tapirs and hunting dogs. Then they headed down past Barclay Court and saw penguins and pelicans and flamingos.

Then they had two doughnuts each on the picnic lawn.

Next it was time to look at the lion cubs that had been born two months before. Sophie took a photo of them every week and put it on her blog.

After that, they went to see some 'Megabugs' in the B.U.G.S. centre. Tom did what he always did: found the red-kneed bird-eating spider and put his nose up against the glass for about ten minutes.

Then it was lunchtime. As they walked into

the Oasis cafe, they saw their parents sitting at their usual table. A tall woman with long red hair was sitting with them.

'Hello, you two,' said Mrs Nightingale. 'Having fun?'

Tom and Sophie nodded.

'Have you been to the reptile house yet?' Mr Nightingale asked.

'No, we're saving that for this afternoon,' said Tom.

'Quite right!' exclaimed the woman. 'Save the best till last! Well, when you get there, ask a member of staff to come and find me.'

'This is Daisy,' said Mr Nightingale. 'She's one of my friends. She runs the reptile house.'

'I want to give you a guided tour. And show you behind the scenes too,' Daisy said.

'Wow!' said Sophie, amazed.

'How come?' asked Tom, astounded.

'To say thank you,' said Daisy. 'Thank you for rescuing those snakes. You've both been very brave and very kind.'

Tom and Sophie looked embarrassed.

'Luckily, nearly all of the snakes were on our collection plan. So that means we can keep them,' said Daisy.

'What's a collection plan?' asked Sophie.

'It's our wish list. Every zoo has a list of animals that it wants to add to its collection,' said Daisy. 'Otherwise we'd end up with three hundred and sixteen zebras and a cormorant. With a collection plan, you have an idea of the species you want to keep and why, and how many of each species.'

'So it's a bit like writing a letter to Father Christmas?' said Sophie. 'You just make a long list of everything you want?'

'Precisely!' said Daisy. 'And on *our* Christmas list there was an inland taipan, an anaconda, a king cobra, a Burmese python, an Antiguan racer, two long-nosed vipers, a black mamba and a banded krait. And thanks to you, we've got the lot!'

'So what do you think, kids?' asked Mr Nightingale. 'Feel like seeing some slimy snakes?'

'They're not slimy, Dad,' Sophie shot back. 'A snake's skin tends to be dry and smooth.'

Daisy burst out laughing. 'They're good, these two! I can see that we're going to become the best of friends!'

Chapter 7

'Now, as I was saying, we don't usually let members of the public back here,' said Daisy as she led Tom and Sophie through a small door in the side of the reptile house, 'so don't tell anyone or I'll feed you to Horace.'

'Is Horace one of your snakes?' asked Tom.

'No, this is Horace,' said Daisy. She introduced a short stocky man in his early sixties with very hairy arms.

'Don't listen to her,' Horace said with a grin. 'I'm a vegetarian.'

'Right, let's show you some snakes,' said Daisy. They left Horace behind and went through

another door. They walked in front of a python's enclosure and then through another small door marked 'PRIVATE'.

They were in a large room, full of busy zookeepers.

'This room is right in the middle of the reptile house,' said Daisy.

Tom and Sophie looked up and around.

'These small hatches in the wall lead directly to the snakes' enclosures,' she went on, pointing at a series of square grey doors. 'We open those when we're cleaning or feeding any of the animals.'

Then Daisy pointed at some boxes and glass cases against one of the walls.

'If we need to take snakes off display,' said Daisy, 'we put them in one of those. The glass cases are for when they're unwell. The boxes are for when they hibernate.'

Next she pointed to a wall covered in tools.

'This is what we use when we're handling snakes,' said Daisy. 'Tongs, hooks and tubes.'

'Do you ever just pick snakes up with your hands?' Tom asked.

Daisy shook her head. 'It's been twenty-five years since anyone was bitten in this zoo and we intend to keep it that way.'

Sophie was looking at the tubes. They were a range of different widths and lengths. 'So what exactly do you use these *for*?' she asked.

'Well, it's funny you should ask that,' Daisy said, 'because one of your mum's friends is coming over in a minute to give one of the adders a blood test. So we can show you.' She looked over her shoulder and called out, 'Horace, can you give us a hand?'

Horace reappeared next to Sophie.

'Now you'll have to stay down here,' said Daisy. 'Me and Horace are going to encourage Rufus, our European adder, into this tube.'

'Why does Horace need to help you?' Tom asked.

'Because whenever we handle a venomous snake, we always go in twos,' said Daisy. 'If anything happens to one of us, the other one can raise the alarm.'

She lowered her voice. 'Actually, Rufus isn't really that venomous, but we don't tell him that. Don't want to hurt his feelings.'

'So how do you make Rufus go into the tube?' Sophie asked.

'We don't need to *make* him!' Dairy said.

'Snakes love little gaps and tunnels,' Horace explained. 'If you put a tube next to them, they'll crawl inside out of curiosity.'

'Once its head is in the tube, we hold its belly so it can't get out,' said Daisy.

The two zookeepers walked up a ramp towards one of the small grey hatches.

Less than a minute later, they were walking back with the snake. 'Stay well back, kids,' said Daisy.

At the same time, one of the vets appeared in the room. He had curly black hair and glasses. Tom and Sophie recognised him as Gavin, one of their mum's colleagues.

They followed Daisy, Horace and Gavin into a small room with a clean white table. Rufus was placed in the centre of the table.

'OK, kids,' Daisy said, 'Gavin here needs to take some blood from Rufus. Guess how he's going to do that.'

'Erm,' said Tom.

'Well, with people,' Sophie said, 'you usually get blood taken from your arm, but I guess Rufus doesn't have one of those.'

'Exactly,' said Daisy, 'but what he does have is a big thick vein running all the way down the middle of his body. And the best place to get to it is here.'

She pointed at his tail.

Gavin smiled and stuck a needle in Rufus's tail.

'Just a little prick, mate,' Gavin said. The adder started to squirm, his head moving from side to side in the tube.

Gavin stroked Rufus gently and the snake calmed down. Then Gavin explained to Sophie and Tom that being in the tube wasn't hurting or distressing Rufus at all.

'So why does he need the blood test?' Sophie asked.

'Well, he's been off his food for a couple of months,' Horace said.

'A couple of months!' exclaimed Sophie.

'Yeah, well, he only eats every couple of weeks,' said Horace, 'so it's like you being off your food for a few days.'

'Oh, I see,' said Sophie.

In the meantime, Gavin was looking at Daisy with a resigned expression.

'I'm not getting any blood,' he said. 'I'll have to go straight for the heart.'

'His heart?' said Sophie, with a concerned look.

'It's nothing to worry about,' Daisy said. 'We do it all the time. It's just a really easy place to get a sample. Only problem is finding it.'

'How come it's hard to find?' Tom said, putting his hand up to his own heart.

'Well, it's easy to find *yours*,' said Daisy. 'It's just under your chest, next to your left arm. But what if you didn't have a chest or a left arm?'

'So how do you find it?' Sophie asked, with

another concerned look at Gavin, who was feeling the snake's body.

'It's about a third of the way along,' Gavin said, looking up at Sophie through his big glasses, 'but it's different for every snake. We have a card telling us about each one. For Rufus, it's about twenty-five centimetres from his head. That's when it's not moving.'

'His heart moves?' said Tom, feeling his own again and looking at the snake on the table.

'Yes, every day it's somewhere slightly different,' said Gavin, pressing a point on Rufus's belly. 'Your heart's kept in the same place by all kinds of muscles and tendons. But Rufus's isn't. It can slide up and down. It means that as I put the needle in that can make the heart slip out of the way.'

'Out of the way?' Sophie repeated.

'Doesn't normally happen though,' Gavin conceded. 'There we are.'

'Got what you need, Gav?' Daisy asked.

'Yes,' said Gavin, injecting a syringe's worth of snake's blood into a small bottle. 'I'll run some tests and let you know the results tomorrow.'

He washed his hands, clipped up his vet's case and left the room.

'Right, let's get Rufus back home,' said Daisy.

After she had returned Rufus to his vivarium, Tom said to Daisy, 'Doesn't Rufus get lonely? You know, being on his own all day?'

'Not really,' said Daisy. 'Most snakes live by themselves, you see. They're not sociable like us. Besides, we have got two other adders if we ever did feel like he needed a friend.'

'Two others?' Tom echoed. 'I've never seen them.'

'You wouldn't have,' Daisy said. 'They're kept upstairs. The zoo generally only displays a fraction of the animals in its collection. We've got dozens of snakes that the public has never seen.'

'Where are they?' Sophie asked.

'I'm about to show you,' Daisy said with a grin. She flicked her hair over her shoulder and led the way out of the large room and back through the reptile house.

Chapter 8

Upstairs, Tom and Sophie found themselves in a large white room full of vivariums of all shapes and sizes. They were arranged in five long rows.

They saw coral snakes and corn snakes, rat snakes and rhinocerous snakes, copperheads and keelbacks.

'So why aren't these snakes on show?' Sophie asked.

'All sorts of reasons,' said Daisy. 'Maybe we've already got one on display. Maybe we haven't got the right vivarium for them. Maybe they're hibernating. Maybe they're pregnant. But, you know, we still love them.'

Tom was staring at a gigantic constrictor in a long clear enclosure.

'That's Bessie,' said Daisy. 'She's twelve metres long. That's probably eight times longer than you! And I think she's hungry.'

Tom took a small step back.

'Don't worry, I didn't mean she'd eat you,' said Daisy. 'I mean it's time to feed her. Want to help?'

Tom and Sophie both grinned and said, 'Yes.'

They spent the next hour helping Daisy with a variety of tasks.

First Tom fed Bessie, dropping a whole defrosted turkey, feathers and all, into her enclosure. They watched the snake stretch her mouth around the bird and swallow it whole.

'She's dislocating her jaw, isn't she?' Sophie said.

'Not quite,' Daisy said. 'Her jaw's on a hinge so she can swing it all the way back. Then she has a tendon in the middle of her chin that can stretch sideways till it's wider than her body.'

'Why doesn't she just chew it?' Tom asked.

'Her teeth are too small to chew anything,' Daisy said.

'But doesn't she have massive fangs?' Tom asked.

'No, she's a constrictor,' Daisy said. 'Only snakes with venom have true fangs. Even if she did have them, most fangs are hollow – so they can squirt venom through the middle. You know, like that needle Gavin was holding? They're no good for mashing up food. Having said that, she still has quite a set of teeth on her and you wouldn't want her to bite you!'

They watched for five minutes: three-quarters of the turkey was still sticking out of Bessie's mouth.

'You can stay till the end if you like,' Daisy said, 'but it may take her a couple of hours to swallow it. You know, Bessie could eat something much bigger than that – even something as big as a Labrador!'

Tom and Sophie stared at the turkey in Bessie's mouth for a few seconds more. Then they followed Daisy to the next vivarium where a corn snake was coiled up in a corner.

'This is Shaun,' said Daisy. 'He's having problems shedding his skin.'

Daisy looked in and saw a strip hanging from the side of his body.

'That's why I put that big pool of water in his vivarium,' said Daisy, 'but I think we might need to give him a bit more help.'

She reached under the vivarium and pulled

out a branch. She
offered the branch
to Sophie and
opened the top of
the vivarium.

'Put the branch
in his pool of water.
He'll be able to rub
himself against that and nudge his skin off.'

Sophie hesitated.

'It's OK,' said Daisy. 'He's a constrictor too.
Won't bite. And he'll only constrict you if you
look like and smell a rat.'

'Watch out then, Soph,' Tom said.

Sophie ignored him and put the branch in the
vivarium.

'How often does he shed?' Sophie asked,
watching Shaun slide towards the branch.

'Every couple of months,' said Daisy.

'Why do they do it?' asked Tom.

'Because snakes keep outgrowing their skin,'
Daisy said. 'They're not like us. They don't get

to eighteen and stop. They grow their whole lives. And their skin doesn't stretch. If they didn't shed their skin, they'd burst out of it.'

'That would be way better,' said Tom.

Next Tom and Sophie helped to clean out a vivarium. Daisy removed the snake with hooks and placed it in another enclosure. Tom and Sophie learned that each vivarium had a heat mat at one end of it, so that the snakes had a hot part (to warm up) and a cold part (to cool down).

'Snakes can be pretty slow in the morning unless they get to a certain temperature,' Daisy explained.

Tom and Sophie changed the substrate on the vivarium floor – pouring in fresh woodchips from a large bag. They also learned how to fit the vivarium lid on securely.

They were looking at a mangrove snake called Clive when Daisy's radio started to crackle.

'Hello, this is Reptiles,' said Daisy. 'Yep, yep, on my way.'

She turned to Tom and Sophie.

'Bet you want to see those snakes you rescued yesterday,' said Daisy.

'Yes!' exclaimed Tom and Sophie.

'Well, that was your mum,' said Daisy. 'They're about to operate on a green mamba. Want to come along?'

Two minutes later they were walking through the zoo on their way to the hospital.

At the door to the hospital they met Gavin again. His big glasses were squares of light in the sunshine.

'We've got some students in from the Royal Veterinary College so you can stand with them in the observation room,' he said, as he opened the door and ushered them inside.

'Will I get a lamp on my head?' Tom whispered to Sophie excitedly.

'We'll just be watching, not operating,' Sophie replied.

'Do you think the mamba will need LOTS of stitches at the end?' Tom asked her.

'Very possibly,' said Sophie.

As they walked into the hospital building, both Tom and Sophie looked around. They'd visited their mother's workplace a few times before, but it still felt like a strange and amazing place.

They passed one treatment room where a vet was peering up a coati's long droopy nose. In the next room, another vet was gently lifting a pelican's wing.

Tom hovered in the doorway of the third room. A vet was unlocking a cabinet, and then unlocking another door inside the cabinet. She pulled out a tranquilliser gun.

'What's she going to shoot?' Tom asked Gavin, as Sophie pulled him away.

'Nothing,' said Gavin. 'She just needs to practise. Shooting a dart into an animal is very tricky. You can be quite some distance away. And you have to hit muscle, not bone, or it can really hurt the animal. So all of us practise on a regular basis.'

'Not Mum, though?' Sophie asked.

'Of course your mum!' said Gavin. 'She's an excellent shot.'

Tom and Sophie looked at each other. Daisy leaned in and said, 'Better do what she says in future, eh?'

Now they had arrived at a large room next to an operating theatre. There were three white screens on one wall, lit from behind by small bulbs.

A split second later, Sophie and Tom's mum walked in, holding a series of X-rays. There were three veterinary students behind her. Their mother already had scrubs on – a gown, hat and mask. She had pulled her mask down under her chin and was explaining something to one of the students.

Mrs Nightingale looked up and smiled at her children, then carried on talking.

'So next up: Gareth the green mamba. Let's have a look at these X-rays,' she said, pinning five of the films side by side on the white screens.

'Normally you just have one X-ray,' Daisy

said quietly to Tom and Sophie, 'but with snakes you have to take one, then move the snake along, take another, move the snake along. Till you've X-rayed all of him. Then you stick the X-rays together.'

'So what's eating Gareth?' Mrs Nightingale asked. 'Or what's Gareth been eating?'

The three students peered at the X-rays. Sophie stood on tiptoes and looked over their shoulders.

A large white circle was visible about halfway along Gareth's body.

'Is it a retained egg?' one of the students asked. 'Maybe she laid all the others, but not that one?'

'Can anyone tell me why that's unlikely?' Mrs Nightingale asked.

The students all looked at each other and then back at the X-rays.

'Because Gareth's not a girl,' Sophie said quietly.

'That's right!' exclaimed Mrs Nightingale. 'The clue's is in the name.'

The students looked at Sophie, and Sophie blushed and looked at the ground.

'Any other guesses?' Mrs Nightingale asked.

'Does she – sorry, he –' began another student. Everyone tittered.

'Could *he* have a tumour?' the student asked.

'That's a better suggestion,' said Mrs Nightingale. 'Anyone agree with that?'

The other two students put their hands up, then put them down again, then put them up again.

'It looks too solid for a tumour,' one of them eventually said.

'Plus, does he have any other symptoms of cancer?' Mrs Nightingale asked.

The students all shook their heads.

'Which leaves . . . ?' Mrs Nightingale asked.

'A foreign body,' said one of the students hesitantly.

'Correct!' Mrs Nightingale said. 'It looks to me like it could be a stone. So can anyone tell me why this most intelligent of creatures has swallowed a stone?'

71

'Could he have thought it was a bird's egg?' one of the students asked.

Mrs Nightingale smiled and shook her head.

Sophie had an idea, but bit her tongue. Daisy could see that Sophie wanted to guess, so nudged her. 'Go on,' Daisy said, 'she won't bite. She ain't a mamba, is she?'

'Maybe,' stammered Sophie, 'maybe he was swallowing his prey. You know, a rat or whatever. But there was a pebble in his enclosure. Underneath the rat. And he swallowed both at the same time. By mistake.'

The students all looked impressed. 'Yeah,' one of them said, 'it has to be that. Definitely.'

'That *is* the right answer,' Mrs Nightingale said. 'Well done, Sophie. Everyone, this is my daughter. And that's my son, Tom. Be nice to them and I'll give you all a distinction.'

The students all said hello and smiled.

'OK,' Mrs Nightingale said. 'Gavin, Daisy, time to scrub up.'

Chapter 9

Tom and Sophie stood behind a glass panel in the operating theatre alongside the student vets.

They could see the operation through the glass and on a large monitor in front of them. Mrs Nightingale was performing the operation and Gavin was assisting. Daisy was standing next to them, ready to advise.

Throughout the procedure Mrs Nightingale was describing what it was she was doing. Her voice came through a large speaker under the monitor. This meant that Tom, Sophie and the students could see and hear everything that was happening to the snake.

'The mamba is now anaesthetised and I am ensuring a free flow of oxygen to the lungs,' said Mrs Nightingale, her voice crackling over the speaker. 'Notice that I am careful to avoid the fangs in case of a reflex bite.'

Tom and Sophie watched the monitor in fascination as their mother pushed a tube down the snake's throat and hooked him up to an oxygen supply, just like a surgeon would with a person.

'Now we make a small incision along the side of the snake. Never cut a snake across its belly or the wound will never heal. Every time it moves, the cut will open up,' said Mrs Nightingale.

Tom and Sophie watched in wonder as their mother made a small neat cut along the side of the snake and the blood seeped out.

'It's red, just like ours,' said Tom.

'Well, what colour did you expect it to be?' Sophie said.

'Green, of course,' said Tom.

'A snake's scales are made out of keratin,' Mrs Nightingale continued. 'Just like our hair and fingernails – so they grow back and heal fairly quickly. Snakes are used to getting cuts and nicks in the wild. Some constrictors even stretch their skin till it bursts when they eat something huge.'

'Grim,' muttered Sophie.

'Their insides are more robust than ours generally,' explained Mrs Nightingale. 'Their organs are used to moving around and squeezing out of the way when something big gets swallowed. And remember, all of their organs are in a long line. They're not side by side like ours. So their right kidney is *under* their left kidney.'

Sophie heard the students next to her whispering and scribbling away on their clipboards.

Soon Mrs Nightingale was removing the stone from the snake's stomach with a pair of surgical forceps.

'You'll be OK, mate. You're doing great,' Daisy whispered to the snake.

Mrs Nightingale dropped the stone into a tin dish with a clink.

'OK, time to close him up,' she said. 'Remember that animals are just like people – the longer you expose their insides to the air, the greater the risk of infection. So any surgery should be as swift as possible.'

'If he swallowed me,' Tom whispered to Sophie, 'and someone cut me out, would I still be alive? Or would I be, like, half digested, with a weird zombie face?'

'Shh, I want to see how Mum does this,' Sophie said.

They watched their mother and Gavin unclamping the snake and stitching him up.

The students continued to sketch and scribble.

One of them was a young woman with long brown hair. She looked across at Sophie and said, 'You want to be a vet like your mum?'

Sophie nodded and said, 'A zoo vet though.

Not a normal vet. I'm not really into cats and gerbils.'

The young woman smiled and said, 'Just into the other hundred million species on the planet? Yeah, me too!'

When the operation was over, Mrs Nightingale came over to Tom and Sophie and said, 'See you back at home, you two.'

Then she left the room with Gavin.

Daisy had taken off her surgical gear and was mopping her brow.

'Man, those things are tense,' she said, 'but he's going to be fine. Now, since we're in the hospital, how would you like to see those snakes you rescued?'

'Seriously?' Sophie said, with a surprised expression.

'I mean, they're in quarantine,' said Daisy, 'so it'll be look-but-don't-touch, but still. Should be good, clean fun.'

'Cool!' Tom said.

They walked along a corridor and then through a pair of double doors.

'Talking of clean fun,' said Daisy, 'first thing we have to do is get clean.'

They were in a small lobby with a washbasin against the wall, rows of boots on the floor, bottles of chemicals on shelves and gowns hanging up on hooks.

'Animals in quarantine are kept completely separate,' said Daisy. 'Different vets, different rooms, different enclosures. Anyone going to see them has to be totally free of germs.'

'Tom's never free of germs,' said Sophie.

'Sophie is a germ,' said Tom.

They scrubbed their hands with grainy blue soap and Daisy made them put on special boots. Then they put on overalls over their clothes before Daisy led them to a small yellow room with vivariums on all sides.

'This is where the snakes will live for the next few months,' said Daisy.

'Are they all OK?' Sophie asked.

'They are now,' said Daisy. 'We rehydrated them all. Some of them had parasites so we've been treating them for that. Some have had medecine. Others have had a special spray on their skin. We're steering clear of him though.'

She pointed to a golden snake with a jet-black head in a large vivarium. It was crawling slowly over a rock. 'He's an inland taipan,' Daisy explained, 'the world's most venomous snake. He's only a metre and a half long, but one bite could kill an adult elephant. Stone dead. In about ten minutes.'

Tom and Sophie peered through the glass.

'And we haven't got the antivenin yet,' Daisy added.

Tom and Sophie stepped back from the glass.

'I know,' Daisy said. 'It's like working with explosives sometimes. Next door we've got an Antiguan racer. One of the world's rarest snakes. Only a few hundred left in the wild. I'm so unbelievably glad you found her.'

Daisy looked at the taipan again, then smiled at Tom and Sophie.

'Over here, we've got your old friend the

king cobra,' she continued. 'Did you know they're cannibals? His primary diet in the wild is other snakes, including cobras. In here he has to make do with mice though, don't you, Colin?'

She turned to the next case along.

'Here's our black mamba,' she said. 'The fastest snake in the world. Reaches speeds of fourteen miles per hour. And here's our married couple. Two long-nosed vipers. A male in that vivarium and a female in that one.'

Sophie looked at the female viper curled up in a corner of the enclosure.

'Are those holes in the vivarium so she can breathe?' Sophie asked.

'Yes, we'd have to move her if she was pregnant though, or her babies could squeeze through those holes when they were born. And talking of babies . . .'

She beckoned Tom and Sophie over to a vivarium next to the door.

'This one is a banded krait,' she said.

Tom and Sophie stared at a long, slender

snake with bright black and yellow stripes. Its head was held back in an S-shape as it investigated a hollowed-out branch.

'She's beautiful,' Sophie murmured.

'Yes, and she laid some eggs this morning,' said Daisy, 'so soon we should have even more of them.'

'Wow!' said Tom, peering through the glass. 'So where's she hiding the eggs?'

'We took them off to incubate them,' said Daisy.

'Don't you let her keep them?' said Tom.

Daisy shook her head.

'It's better if we take them,' she said. 'You see, snakes aren't always the best parents in the world. Normally they lay their eggs in a nice spot and leave them. As soon as the eggs hatch, they scarper. Partly because, if they stayed around, they might get eaten by their own mum and dad.'

'Whoa!' Tom said. 'And I thought Mum and Dad were annoying!'

'Plus, you know,' Daisy went on, 'baby snakes can look after themselves. They're born with all their venom. They may be only a fraction of the size of their mothers, but their bite is just as deadly. You'd never guess from looking at them though. Come on, I'll show you.'

Tom and Sophie could barely contain their excitement.

Daisy led them down a corridor, through a series of treatment rooms and into a laboratory lined with small plastic incubators humming gently.

'Look, look, those ones have just hatched,' Daisy whispered.

'Are they from the banded krait?' Sophie asked.

'No, they're from our false water cobra,' said Daisy.

Tom and Sophie were looking at six small white eggs, longer and softer than chickens' eggs. Three of the eggs had a snake's head sticking out of the top. Two others just had tongues flickering in and out.

'When are they actually going to come out?'
Tom asked.

'Oh, they might sit like that for a few days,'
said Daisy, 'biding their time. First they just stick
their tongue out, like those two, smelling and
sensing what's out there, checking for predators.
Then they stick their head out, taking in the
scenery. The weirdest thing is, they're each
about twenty centimetres long in there.'

'No way!' exclaimed Tom.

'Really?' said Sophie.

'I know it sounds impossible,' said Daisy. 'I mean – how do they curl up so tightly and fit themselves into that small egg? But somehow they do. And why? Because snakes are incredible, kids. The most incredible animals on the planet.'

Chapter 10

That evening, on the houseboat, all Tom and Sophie could talk about was snakes. How snakes keep growing their whole lives and how their hearts are in a different place every day and how they can't even move in the morning until they warm up. It was all Mrs Nightingale could do to get them to eat their dinner.

'And after we saw you do the operation,' said Sophie, 'we saw the snakes in quarantine too.'

'Yeah,' said Tom. 'One of the ones we saved was pregnant!'

'And we saw some other eggs that a snake

had laid, and their heads were poking out,' said Sophie.

'All right, all right,' said Mr Nightingale, 'we get it. You had a good day. But can we talk about something else now?'

'How about Komodo dragons?' suggested Tom.

'No,' said Mrs Nightingale. 'No more reptiles.'

'What about poisonous tree frogs?' Sophie asked.

'Or amphibians,' said Mrs Nightingale.

'OK, let's talk about humans,' said Sophie, 'specifically me and Tom. When can we get a snake?'

Mr Nightingale smiled and groaned at the same time.

'We're going to need a bigger boat,' he said.

Later on, Sophie was reading about Antiguan racers on the internet. Tom was sitting behind her on the sofa, reading *The Little Book of Big Snakes*.

'I can't believe that man on the barge had stolen an Antiguan racer,' Sophie said, pointing at a webpage. 'He must have known they're almost extinct.'

'He was a slimeball all right,' Tom said, still looking at his book.

'Still, it says here there's a breeding programme in Antigua,' Sophie added. 'They're trying to build their numbers up again. We should tell Daisy about it.'

'Yeah, OK,' said Tom. 'I was going to tell Daisy something else too.'

'What?' asked Sophie.

'Well, I was reading about long-nosed vipers in here –' he held his book open on a double-page spread of photos depicting a long-nosed viper swallowing a shrew. 'Apparently it's really hard to tell when they're pregnant, but I think that viper in quarantine might have been. Look at this picture. They're usually wider than a regular snake, right? But here it's even fatter.'

'Maybe,' said Sophie.

'And think about it,' said Tom. 'It was in one of those pillowcases with a male long-nosed viper. You remember what happened when we bought Felicity the ferret a friend and Georgina turned out to be a George. We got baby ferrets. I reckon the same would happen with snakes!'

'We'll tell her in the morning then,' said Sophie.

'Maybe we should tell her now,' said Tom. 'Don't you remember? Those breathing holes were pretty big. And look at this picture.'

Tom pointed at a photo of a long-nosed viper snakelet.

'They can't be more than five millimetres wide,' said Tom. 'They're much smaller than the holes on the box.'

'So what?' replied Sophie. 'Even if she lays eggs, they're not going to hatch overnight.'

'She doesn't lay eggs,' said Tom, 'she's ovov— ovoviv— this word here.'

Sophie said, 'Ovoviviparous.'

'It means she gives birth to live snakes in little sacs,' said Tom. 'They wriggle out of the sacs and off they go.'

'They'll be able to escape,' whispered Sophie.

'And they'll be just as venomous as their mum from the moment they're born,' Tom added.

Tom and Sophie ran into the kitchen, where their parents were washing up.

'Mum! Dad! We need Daisy's phone number! Now!' declared Sophie.

'Oh, blooming henry, what now?' Mr Nightingale groaned.

'The zoo's closed,' said Mrs Nightingale.

Tom and Sophie explained.

'You're sure about this?' Mr Nightingale asked.

'Ring Daisy,' Mrs Nightingale said. 'I'll go and take a look.'

She picked up a torch and Tom and Sophie walked quickly with their mother along the towpath.

Slicing through the darkness with the torch's beam, they crossed the bridge that led to the zoo and went through the staff entrance.

Horace was already waiting to meet them at the reptile house.

'Daisy just phoned me,' he said. 'It's funny, cos I was just about to check on that viper. I had the same feeling as you two.'

'Were we right?' asked Tom.

Horace nodded. 'I've just been in. I reckon she's about to pop. Give her another hour or so.'

'I knew it!' exclaimed Tom.

'I've replaced the metal grille on her enclo-sure with a sheet of glass,' said Horace. 'If those snakelets had wriggled out, that would NOT have been nice. You did good, kids.'

'Can we watch, Mum? Go on, go on,' Tom pleaded.

Mrs Nightingale looked at her watch. 'Well, it's technically way past your bedtime,' she said.

'But we did stop those snakes from escaping,' Tom said, 'sort of. Horace would have been bitten to death. Maybe.'

Mrs Nightingale sighed and nodded.

So Tom and Sophie got to watch Lydia the long-nosed viper give birth to seven beautiful slithery venomous snakelets. They plopped out in slippery sacs and soon burst through.

Daisy arrived just in time to see the happy event. She quickly took the snakelets out of the vivarium with a mini snake hook.

Mrs Nightingale inspected them through the glass and said, 'They look happy and healthy. We can have a better look at them all in the morning. Don't forget to weigh and measure them, Daisy.'

She turned to look at Tom and Sophie. 'Bed!'

Chapter 11

The summer flew by, with lots more weekends at the zoo and lots more trips to see Daisy at the reptile house. Daisy would always give Tom and Sophie updates about the snakes in quarantine.

Tom would ask about the baby long-nosed vipers and Daisy would tell him how long they were now and how many mice she had fed them that week.

Sophie would ask about the Antiguan racer and Daisy would talk about the Antiguan rescue project and how the zoo wanted to reintroduce their racer back into the wild.

Then one day Daisy turned to the children.

'The snakes will be out of quarantine in a fort-night, you know,' she said. 'We're going to throw a big party and introduce them to the world. Want to come as guests of honour?'

Tom and Sophie couldn't believe their ears. 'Yes!' they said.

'So,' Daisy said, 'it'll be an early-evening thing. We'll invite the press and lots of VIPs. We're making new enclosures for the snakes now. The reptile house is about to get a lot bigger!'

That evening, Tom and Sophie talked to their parents about the snake celebrations.

'Daisy says we're going to be guests of honour!' Sophie said.

'That's great news,' said Mrs Nightingale. 'Me and your dad are on duty that evening, so we can all go together.'

'Can we stay late?' Tom asked. 'You know, really late. Like midnight!'

'It finishes at nine, Tom,' Sophie said. 'What are we going to do for three more hours?'

The following Saturday, Tom and Sophie were watching the penguins being fed when Daisy tapped Sophie on the shoulder.

'Hey, you two,' she said. 'I've got a TV reporter coming to talk to me at lunchtime. He wants to meet the people who found the snakes. That means you!'

'TV?' Sophie said, looking suddenly nervous. 'We're going to be on TV?'

'What show's it for?' Tom said. 'What channel's it on?'

'I don't know – it'll be for some news programme,' Daisy said. 'BBC or ITV, I suppose.'

'Wow,' said Tom. 'I'll be a national hero. Maybe even a *national treasure*.'

'I need to put on a different top,' Sophie said, 'and sort my hair out.'

'Whatever makes you happy,' said Daisy. 'See you at the reptile house at one.'

They raced back to *The Ark*, got ready in record time and arrived at the reptile house at exactly 12.45, looking very smart and very excited.

'Right, I'll do the first bit,' Sophie said, 'about the man in the boat.'

'And I'll do the next bit,' said Tom, 'about finding the cobra.'

'OK, then I'll do the bit about the vets and the fire engine arriving.'

'But hang on, that means you get two bits and I get one.'

'But you're doing the finding the cobra bit,' said Sophie. 'That's the best bit.'

'So doing the best bit is the same as doing two boring bits?' Tom asked.

'Yes,' Sophie said.

'I suppose that does make sense,' Tom admitted.

'Hello, you two,' Daisy said, appearing in front of them. 'Worked out your story?'

'Yes,' they both said.

'This is Martin,' Daisy said, gesturing at a man in a suit. Behind him there was a cameraman, and a woman holding a fluffy microphone on a long stick.

'So these are the children that saved the day,' Martin, the reporter, said. 'Lovely. Let's do the interview over there. With that big snake behind you.'

'That's a Burmese python,' Tom said. 'It's one of the six biggest snakes in the world.'

They went and stood in front of the python's vivarium.

The reporter began by talking directly to camera.

'In just a week's time, the reptile house at London Zoo will be transformed. A dozen new snakes will join the permanent collection. But what's interesting is *how* these snakes arrived here. They were found by two young children, Tom and Sophie Nightingale, after they were abandoned on the Regent's Canal by a notorious animal smuggler. The smuggler is now safely behind bars. Tom and Sophie, however, are with me here now. Tom, Sophie, hello.'

'Hello,' said Sophie.

'So we were coming home from school and we saw this scary-looking bloke with a snake round his neck,' Tom began.

'Whoa right there, Tom,' the reporter said. 'Let me get a question out first.'

The woman with the fluffy microphone lowered it to the ground.

'Oh, OK,' Tom said. 'Do I have to say that bit again then?'

'In a minute, yes,' said the reporter, gesturing to the woman with the microphone.

'OK. So, Tom, Sophie, tell me how you came across this sack of slimy snakes.'

'Snakes aren't slimy,' said Sophie quickly. 'Their skin is dry and smooth.'

'OK, OK,' said the reporter. The woman put down the microphone again. 'Don't worry if I make mistakes. Just answer the questions as best you can.'

'You can't call snakes slimy though,' Tom said. 'Mum will never forgive us. By the way, can we say hello to Mum and Dad on the telly?'

'Maybe, yes, at some point,' the reporter said, looking slightly impatient, 'OK, how about slithery snakes? Is that OK?'

Tom and Sophie looked at each other.

'I suppose they DO slither,' said Sophie.

'Unless they're sidewinders,' Tom said.

'That's true,' said Sophie, 'but even they slither *sometimes*.' She turned to the reporter. 'Slithery is acceptable.'

So the reporter started again. Sophie went first, talking about the man on the boat. Tom talked about his face-to-face encounter with a king cobra.

'And now they've got a new home here in the zoo,' the reporter concluded. 'Those snakes are very lucky to have met you two.'

'We're lucky we met them!' Tom said.

'Snakes are mind-blowing, seriously!' Sophie exclaimed.

Tom and Sophie both talked for another five minutes, raving about all the amazing things they'd discovered about snakes, while the reporter and the cameraman and the boom mike operator watched and smiled.

Chapter 12

The following Saturday was the big day. Tom and Sophie visited the reptile house at lunchtime to see how preparations were going. Tom had his best friend, Freddy, with him. Sophie had her best friend, Jemima, with her.

Freddy and Jemima were still dubious about snakes.

'Can we see the hippos after?' Jemima asked.

'Yeah, and the gorillas,' said Freddy.

'Just give snakes a chance,' said Sophie. 'You'll see how friendly they are.'

'Look,' said Jemima, 'one of my rules is not to make friends with anything that wants to eat me. Call me crazy, but that's just how it is.'

When they got to the reptile house, Daisy was standing by the entrance, talking anxiously to a woman with a long flowery dress and glasses.

'We can still go ahead,' said Daisy. 'Who cares about a few posters?'

'It's not just posters,' said the woman with the flowery dress. 'It's all of our publicity material. Oh, this is awful. We've told everyone that

we're having a grand opening. And now it will look like we've made no effort at all. I'm sorry, but we have to call it off.'

Tom and Sophie overheard what the woman with short hair had said. 'What's going on?' Sophie asked.

'Hi, kids,' Daisy said. 'This is Lucy, the zoo's Head of Publicity. She was expecting all the materials for the event to arrive yesterday. But apparently they're stuck in the post office in Camden.'

'Why can't you just go and pick them up?' Tom asked.

'It's the Spirit of Camden parade today,' Daisy said. 'They're not letting any cars through. The roads are blocked off.'

'Can't someone walk?' Sophie asked.

'I don't think there's time. And even if there was, I don't think I could carry it all,' Lucy said. She looked at her watch. 'It needs to get here in an hour, or we won't have time to put every-thing up.'

'What is everything?' Freddy asked.

'A banner for the outside of the reptile house,' said Lucy, 'posters for inside. We've got snake badges and pencils to give out. And snake masks to sell in the shop. Plus leaflets full of snake facts.'

'Sounds cool,' Freddy said.

'It would be, if they were here,' said Lucy. 'I'm sorry, everyone, but I've decided. It's off. Cancelled. The snakes will have to meet the public another day.'

'But – hang on,' Tom stammered. 'You can't –'

'Hundreds of people are coming,' Sophie said.

'It's been in all the papers,' Tom said, 'and on telly. We told that reporter all about it.'

Sophie thought for a second and said quickly, 'What if we fetched the materials? And got them here in an hour? Would you still cancel?'

Lucy looked surprised. 'Of course not, but how are you going to do it? I've told you, the roads are closed. And there's loads to carry.'

'Just let us worry about that,' said Sophie. 'If

106

you give us whatever papers we need, we'll get everything for you. Trust us . . . we can do it.'

Lucy hesitated, then she seemed to make a decision. 'All right then,' she said, handing Sophie an official-looking card with delivery information on. 'See you in back here in an hour.'

'So you won't tell anyone it's cancelled, will you?' said Tom, grabbing Freddy and following his sister out of the zoo.

'Not if you're sure you can do it,' said Lucy.

'We are!' said Sophie. 'See you soon!'

As they walked along the Outer Circle of Regent's Park, Tom turned to his sister. 'So what's your plan then, Soph?'

'Er, I haven't massively got one,' said Sophie.

'What?!' cried Tom. 'But you just promised we'd get everything here in an hour!'

'Yes, and if you keep quiet and let me think, we might just do it,' Sophie said. She started walking more quickly. 'OK, first we've got to get to the post office and pick everything up.

But the streets are closed and full of people. So what's the quickest way through?'

'Military vehicle?' suggested Jemima.

'Being shot from a cannon?' said Freddy.

'No,' replied Sophie. 'Skateboards.'

'Yes!' exclaimed Tom. 'Me and Freddy are world class.'

'You're going to have to be,' said Sophie. 'Plus you'll need rucksacks to carry everything.'

'But hang on,' Freddy said, 'Camden's over that way. What about when we get to Gloucester Gate? You're not allowed to skate-board in that part of the park. We'll have to walk.'

'That's where me and Jemima come in,' said Sophie. 'We're both really good at running. I usually win the hundred metres and Jemima wins the two hundred and four hundred.'

'Which are way harder, I might add,' said Jemima.

'So we'll be waiting by Gloucester Gate,' said Sophie. 'You hand the rucksacks over to us, and we'll run through the park and get everything to the reptile house.'

'OK,' Tom said.

'All right,' said Freddy.

'So what are you waiting for? Go and get your skateboards and the biggest rucksacks you can find,' said Sophie, 'then head for the post office and show them this.'

Tom took the document that Sophie was holding and then ran down the towpath towards *The Ark*, with Freddy following close behind.

'Right,' Sophie said, turning to Jemima, 'we'll need to get into our running gear. And start warming up.'

'You seriously think those two chumps can do this?' said Jemima. 'They're about five years old.'

'They're nine,' said Sophie. 'And if anyone can cut through a thousand people marching, it's two small boys on skateboards . . .'

Within five minutes, Tom and Freddy were on their skateboards, whizzing down Parkway

and into Camden.
They were both
wearing red ruck-
sacks that were
almost as big as they
were.

The road was closed off and
the parade hadn't started yet, so the
street was empty, the pavements were clear,
and the boys were able to go at top speed.

As they turned left into Camden High Street,
people were starting to gather, carrying banners
and dressed in brightly coloured outfits. Tom
and Freddy had to slow down.

'Remember that time when we were in the
park, skateboarding like snakes?' Tom said.
'Well, that's what we have to do here. Move in
an S-shape. Weave around people. It's called a
serpentine movement.'

'OK, cool,' said Freddy.

Tom started to move his skateboard in an
S-shape, winding past groups of people and

zigzagging between boxes of costumes. Freddy copied him. Soon they were going at a good speed again.

Tom looked at his watch. 'It's taken us five minutes so far. Record time.'

A minute later, and they had arrived at the post office. They went up to the counter and showed the woman there the document from the zoo. The woman looked at the document and looked at Tom and Freddy and looked at the document again. Then she sniffed and started piling up boxes and bags on her side of the counter before sliding up a pane of glass next to her. She pushed everything through it to Tom and Freddy's side.

Tom and Freddy looked at the boxes and bags and then looked at each other.

'We'll never be able to carry all that,' said Freddy.

Then the woman behind the counter started piling up more boxes and bags on her side of the counter. She slid up the glass again and said,

'Make some space over there, lads.'

Tom and Freddy lifted a couple of the boxes on to the floor. One had snake key rings in; one had snake badges.

'OK, we'll have to do this in two lots,' said Tom.

'But we haven't got time,' said Freddy. 'That Lucy said an hour.'

'So we'll have to go twice as fast,' Tom said, 'Let's start by putting these two boxes of posters into my rucksack. You put that banner in yours. It should fit.'

Tom explained to the woman behind the counter that they'd be collecting the rest in fifteen minutes.

'Haven't you got a grown-up to help you, lads?' she asked.

Tom decided it was easiest to lie. 'Yes, my dad's outside. And my mum. And my Uncle Sylvester.'

'And my Auntie Mavis,' added Freddy.

'Good job too,' the woman said.

Outside, the parade had started. People were banging drums and singing.

Tom and Freddy got back on their skateboards, but at first they found it hard to adjust to the weight on their backs. They had to move their feet further apart and lean further forward. Each of them fell off the first time they tried to change direction.

'This is useless, Tom,' said Freddy, 'and dangerous.'

'We'll be fine,' said Tom. 'Imagine we're snakes that have just eaten a massive meal!'

'But they just crawl under a hedge and sleep it off,' said Freddy.

'OK, so imagine a tiger's coming,' said Tom, 'and we *have* to move. Come on, serpentine motion. The S-shape.'

'I can't do it,' protested Freddy. He crouched lower and moved his feet even further apart. He

jolted down from the pavement on to the street without falling off.

'I can do it,' he said with a smile.

As the crowds moved further down the street, Tom and Freddy had to move in even tighter loops, turning more often, twisting more sharply. This, plus the weight on their back, meant that they were moving constantly on their boards, squatting down, standing up, leaning left, diving right.

Sweat was pouring off their brows.

'Keep going,' Tom said, looking at his watch.

Up ahead, Tom and Freddy saw that the road had been completely cordoned off, with a police officer blocking the way.

'Down here,' Tom said, pointing at an alley with a set of steps that led down to the Outer Circle of the park.

'I've only ever done a couple of steps before,' said Freddy.

'We're going to be sidewinders,' said Tom. 'Have you ever seen the way they move? They leap down sand dunes, chucking themselves in the air, landing on their sides for a split second, then jumping again.'

'Seriously?'

'Come on, imagine you're a sidewinder,' said Tom.

Tom pictured a long, sandy-coloured sidewinder in his head, then swivelled his skateboard sideways and started to leap down the steps.

Freddy looked at Tom and then closed his eyes. 'Sidewinder. Sidewinder . . .' he whispered.

He followed Tom down the steps, lifting his feet and his board with them, jumping again and again.

Down at the bottom, they grinned at each other.

'Now, we have to move recti— er . . . recti-linear, I think,' said Tom.

'Rectangular?'

'Rectilinear. It means a straight line,' said Tom. 'Snakes can move straight forward like caterpillars too, but fast. Come on – last one to Gloucester Gate is a mongoose.'

They powered forward with their skateboards, straight along the pavement, thrusting themselves onward with their right feet, then using both feet on the skateboard to push and tilt and pivot, depending on the shape and smoothness and angle of the paving stones.

In their heads, both of them were snakes now. They might have looked like boys, but they were actually anacondas whipping through the water, boas sliding through the jungle ferns, banded flying snakes gliding through the air.

They reached Gloucester Gate in two minutes. Sophie and Jemima were waiting in their running gear.

'Wow, that was seriously fast,' said Sophie. 'We're going to make it!'

'I know, but . . . but . . . this is only half . . . of it. We've got to go back for ev— everything else,' Tom said, trying to get his breath.

'Blimey, Tom,' said Sophie, 'we'll never do it. We've only got half an hour left or Lucy will cancel.'

'We can do it,' said Tom. 'Take the rucksacks to the zoo and bring them back to us empty. We'll be waiting. Then we'll go and get the rest.'

'We're sna . . . snakes,' said Freddy, still panting. 'Snakes can do anything.'

'OK,' said Sophie. 'It has to be worth a try.'

Sophie and Jemima strapped the rucksacks to their backs and started to run.

They sprinted across the grass, focusing on the outline of the zoo in the distance.

After about a hundred metres, Jemima started to flag.

'It's this rucksack,' she said. 'It weighs a ton.'

'Just imagine a snake is chasing you,' Sophie said, breathing heavily. 'A black mamba. They can go up to fourteen miles per hour.' She started to run faster.

Jemima frowned and sped up too. 'That black

mamba ain't going to catch this gazelle.'

'Come on,' said Sophie, 'it's quicker to squeeze through here.' She pointed at a hedgerow with a small hole in the middle and slipped through. Jemima followed, but halfway through the hood of her sweatshirt snagged on a branch. She tugged it but it got even more tangled up.

'OK,' she said. 'Time to shed my skin.'

She wriggled out of her sweatshirt and left it in the bush.

'I'll come back for it later,' she said.

She started to run again in her T-shirt.

Within two minutes the two girls were standing in front of the reptile house. Daisy was standing by the entrance, looking stunned, as Sophie took the boxes out of her rucksack. Jemima took the banner and a bag of snake paperweights out of hers.

'I think Lucy is phoning the press to cancel now,' said Daisy. 'I'll run over and find her. Hopefully I can stop her.'

'We'd better get the rest,' said Sophie. 'Come on, Jemima.'

They ran back to where Tom and Freddy were waiting. They were slower this time even though the bags were empty; they both got a stitch and their legs started to feel wobbly, but they kept running.

They handed the rucksacks to Tom and Freddy. 'Quick as you can,' said Sophie.

Tom and Freddy sped off on their skateboards.

This time when they reached the High Street, the two boys stopped. The parade was in full swing and there was no way they could fight through the crowds. Then they saw a group of people in a Chinese dragon costume emerging from a restaurant. Twenty pairs of legs stuck out of the bottom of a long red shaggy tube. The people in the costume started to wriggle like a snake through the crowd.

'Let's tuck in behind them,' said Tom.

So they followed directly behind the

Chinese dragon, twisting and turning on their skateboards whenever the dragon twisted and turned.

'There's the post office!' said Freddy.

Tom and Freddy leapt on to the pavement and into the post office. It was deserted now. Everyone was either watching or taking part in the parade. Quickly they loaded up their rucksacks with the remaining boxes and bags before dashing back into the street.

'There's the tail end of the parade,' said Tom. 'Come on.'

They sped along the pavement and around the back of the parade. There was a ramp back on to the opposite pavement.

Tom whizzed up the ramp as fast as he could, lifting his skateboard up to his backside as he flew through the air, pushing it back down again as he landed in front of a shop doorway.

Freddy whooped and did the same.

'Bonus points for a mid-air trick!' he exclaimed.

Two minutes later they were handing the rucksacks over to Sophie and Jemima.

The two girls sprinted across the park even faster than before and wriggled through the hole in the hedge.

'I'll need to hibernate after all this,' said Jemima, panting.

When they reached the reptile house, Lucy and Daisy were waiting for them.

'Thank you, thank you, thank you,' said Lucy. 'I can't believe you did it.'

Sophie and Jemima, exhausted, swung their rucksacks on to the floor.

'How did you manage it, girls?' Daisy asked, 'I'm proud of you.'

'Well, we sort of . . . kind of . . .' Sophie stammered.

'We pretended snakes were chasing us,' Jemima said. 'Black mambas, to be precise.'

At that moment, Tom and Freddy arrived

with their skateboards under their arms.

'Did we make it?' Tom asked.

'You made it,' said Lucy, 'and you made my day as well!'

Chapter 13

It was a fantastic party.

The reptile house looked amazing. There were posters on every wall and a long banner draped over the entrance. Outside, Lucy was giving out badges and bookmarks and fact sheets.

Tom and Sophie were standing by the new enclosures, looking at the snakes they had rescued.

'Is Clarence OK?' Tom asked, pointing at the anaconda.

'Yes, he's just about to shed,' Sophie said. 'That's why his eyes are a bit glazed.'

'What about Louise?' Tom asked. 'She doesn't seem herself.'

He was gesturing at the Burmese python.

'She's just digesting a rabbit,' said Sophie. 'That's why she's a bit spaced.'

'OK, phew,' Tom said, looking relieved.

Then Sophie glanced at the Antiguan racer and sighed.

'What is it?' Tom asked. 'Is something wrong with Jenny?'

'No, no, it's just . . .'

'It's just what?' Tom asked.

'Daisy said she's been in touch with that rescue project I mentioned. You know, the one in Antigua – where they reintroduce snakes like her back into the wild.'

'Oh, OK,' said Tom.

'Well, they're going to take her,' said Sophie. 'She'll be heading back home in two weeks.'

'Oh,' said Tom, also looking slightly sad. 'Just as we'd started to get to know her.'

'Yeah, I know,' said Sophie, 'but I suppose it's the best thing for her. It's a great programme; they've built the numbers up from fifty to five hundred.'

Then they heard a voice behind them.

'I wondered where you two had got to,' said Mrs Nightingale. She had Grandad with her.

'Can I tell them?' Grandad said. 'Can I tell them now? Go on, Katie, let me tell them.'

'OK, OK,' said their mum, rolling her eyes.

'Terrific news,' said Grandad. 'You know that this racer snake is off to Antigua? Well, your mother's been chosen to accompany her. You know, it's important that she has a vet with her when she's settling in.'

'Oh, OK, that's good,' said Sophie. 'Good for you, Mum.'

'And we're all going with her!' exclaimed Grandad, holding up five tickets.

Tom and Sophie looked at each other in disbelief.

'Well, we thought it was a good excuse for a family holiday,' said Mrs Nightingale. 'We could all do with a bit of a rest. And it's so beautiful out there, and you've both done so much to help her get back to full health.'

'I can't believe it!' cried Sophie, running over to give her mum a hug.

'Is this for real?' exclaimed Tom.

Grandad clapped his hands, looking equally excited. 'I've only been to the Caribbean once, but my word, I've never forgotten it! And the snakes that live out there . . . You know what, once I saw a man mending a car by the side of

the road when a boa slunk out of the forest and started to coil itself round him! The man kept tinkering under the bonnet while the snake crept up his leg. Once it got to the point where the snake was starting to squeeze, the man calmly uncoiled it, starting from the tail. Then he carried on working. Marvellous! Man and snake living in perfect harmony.'

'So,' Mrs Nightingale said, looking at Tom and Sophie, 'want to come along?'

Tom and Sophie looked at each other with a grin.

'Well, I suppose we *are* snake experts now,' Sophie said, putting her arm round her brother's shoulder. 'It makes sense for us to be there, doesn't it?'

'That's just what I was thinking,' said Mrs Nightingale.

'Excellent,' said Grandad, clapping his hands together. 'You two are snake crazy just like your grandad. Here's to having snakes on the brain!'

'Snakes on the brain!' exclaimed Tom.

'Snakes on the brain!' echoed Sophie.

'And the worst thing is,' Mrs Nightingale said, looking at them all with a smile, 'I don't think there's a cure for it . . .'

Zoological Society of London

ZSL London Zoo is a very famous part of the
Zoological Society of London (ZSL).

For almost two hundred years, we have been
working tirelessly to provide hope and a
home to thousands of animals.

And it's not just the animals at ZSL's Zoos in
London and Whipsnade that we are caring for.
Our conservationists are working in more than
50 countries to help protect animals in the wild.

But all of this wouldn't be possible without your help.
As a charity we rely entirely on the generosity of our
supporters to continue this vital work.

By buying this book, you have made an essential
contribution to help protect animals.
Thank you.

Find out more at **zsl.org**

More amazing behind-the-scenes animal action
at London Zoo
with the Nightingale family!

Run! The Elephant Weighs a Ton!
by Adam Frost

The animal-mad Nightingale family are charging out
of town towards a jumbo-sized mystery. Their animal
friends need them. Whoa! What a fright for the new baby
elephant. Something just isn't right. It's up to Tom and
Sophie to find out what!

Available September 2012

Turn the page for a taster of exciting
adventures in the realm of the
Amur tiger in

Paw Prints in the Snow
by Sally Grindley

Joe and his family are in Russia on the trail of one of the
world's rarest creatures, the beautiful Amur tiger.

Exploring a vast, freezing nature reserve, Joe comes closer
to the tigers than he ever imagined – and is drawn into a
daring mission to rescue an injured cub . . .

OUT NOW

Chapter 1

'What's it like putting your arm up a cow's bottom?' Joe Brook asked.

'Warm and squelchy.' Binti, his mother, grinned.

'You wouldn't catch me doing it.' Joe pulled a face.

He was standing on the bottom rung of some metal fencing inside a barn on Mike Downs's farm. His mother was the other side of the fence, dressed in her green overalls and wellington boots, her breath coiling upwards like steam from a kettle as she leant against the cow's rear. Joe watched as she pulled her arm out and removed the long plastic glove that covered most of it.

'It's not much fun for the cow, either,' she said.

'If I was going to be a vet, I'd only want to look after small animals like cats – or wild animals like elephants, because that would be cool.'

'So you think some of what I do is cool then, Joe?'

Binti smiled as she opened the gate and left the cow's enclosure. Most of her work was as an international wildlife vet, but when she was at home she sometimes helped out if called upon by other vets in the area.

'You might have to put your arm up an elephant's bottom too, you know,' she said.

'What for?'

'To find out if a female is pregnant, or perhaps to check for digestive problems. Pretty much the same as for a cow.'

'Well, I wouldn't mind so much if it was an elephant, because they're exciting and I'm half Tanzanian. Cows are boring.'

'Not to a bull they're not.' Binti laughed as she scrubbed her hands. 'Come on, it's dinner time.'

'I'm glad Dad does the cooking, knowing where your hands have just been.' Joe smirked.

His mother cuffed him gently.

Joe shivered as they left the barn. It had become dark and very chilly. They headed back towards the farmhouse, where Mike Downs greeted them on the doorstep. Through a window Joe could see a fire burning brightly and wished he were sitting in front of it.

'I can't find anything abnormal, Mike,' said Binti, 'but I'll send a stool sample off to the lab and see if they come up with anything. In the meantime, just keep an eye on her and give me a call if you're at all worried.'

'Thanks, Binti. I'll try not to disturb your weekend any further.'

'It's all part of the job, Mike. We can't expect animals to fall sick only on weekdays.'

'Are you going to follow in your mum's

footsteps when you're older, young man?' The farmer winked at Joe.

'My son doesn't like getting his hands dirty, do you, Joe?' Binti smiled. 'Right, we ought to make a move. Bye, Mike.'

She linked her arm through Joe's. They walked quickly over to their four-by-four and clambered in.

'Turn the heating up, Mum,' said Joe. 'It's got really cold.'

Binti switched on the engine and played with the dials. 'You'll have to get used to the cold where we're going,' she said, shooting him a glance to watch his reaction.

Joe looked puzzled. 'We're going home for dinner, aren't we?'

'But what about when you break up for half-term?' Binti questioned.

Joe detected a whiff of excitement. 'I know,' he said. 'We're going to Antarctica!'

'Not quite,' said Binti. 'But we *are* going to Russia.'

'Russia?' Joe wasn't sure how to react. 'Why are we going to Russia?'

'I'm going to help train some of the young vets over there in how to anaesthetize tigers.'

'But there aren't any tigers in Russia, are there?' said Joe. 'I thought they were all in India and Sumatra.'

'There are Amur tigers in Russia. They're the biggest, and there are very few left.'

Russia had sounded like a boring place to spend half-term – until Binti mentioned tigers. Now Joe couldn't think of anything better, even if it was going to be cold . . .